LET'S WORK IT OUT™

How to deal with JEALOUSY

Jonathan Kravetz

PowerKiDS press™
New York

Published in 2007 by The Rosen Publishing Group, Inc.
29 East 21st Street, New York, NY 10010

First Edition

Editor: Jennifer Way
Book Design: Ginny Chu
Layout Design: Kate Laczynski

Photo Credits: Cover, p. 1 © Jerome Tisne/Getty Images; pp. 4, 6, 8, 10, 14 Shutterstock.com; pp. 12, 16, 20 © Royalty-Free/Corbis; p. 18 © www.istockphoto.com/Maartje van Caspel.

Library of Congress Cataloging-in-Publication Data

Kravetz, Jonathan.
  How to deal with jealousy / Jonathan Kravetz. — 1st ed.
      p. cm. — (Let's work it out)
  Includes index.
  ISBN-13: 978-1-4042-3674-5 (library binding)
  ISBN-10: 1-4042-3674-0 (library binding)
  1. Jealousy—Juvenile literature. I. Title.
  BJ1535.J4K73 2007
  152.4'8—dc22
                                    2006029634

Manufactured in the United States of America

Contents

Jealousy can bring up lots of different feelings, such as anger or sadness.

What Is Jealousy?

Imagine that you have a teacher whom you like very much. Then a new kid **joins** the class and your teacher starts to pay more attention to her or him. This might make you feel jealous.

Jealousy can happen when you are afraid someone will take something from you that you want, such as someone's friendship. It also happens when you want something another person has, such as a toy or clothes. Jealousy can make people feel or act angry and **upset**.

A friend might make you feel jealous if she shows off when she beats you at something.

Everyone Feels Jealous Sometimes

It is natural to feel jealous sometimes. Adults struggle with jealousy just as much as children. Jealousy can strike even when everything in your life seems to be going well. Have you ever found it hard to feel happy for other people when something good happened to them? That is jealousy getting hold of you!

It is important to learn how to control your feelings of jealousy. If you do not, feelings of jealousy can make you feel very bad.

You may not win every swim meet in which you compete, and that may make you feel jealous of the winner.

Competition

Sometimes you may feel jealous when you **compete**. Imagine that you want to be the fastest runner at school, but you keep losing to another kid. This might make you jealous of the better runner. It could lead to **arguments** or fights if you let your jealousy make you feel angry. You might also find it hard to **cheer** for your friends when they are running. This is a very common kind of jealousy.

Remember that no one wins every time he or she competes. It is okay to lose, as long as you try your hardest.

Sometimes you may feel jealous when you have to compete with other students for your teacher's attention.

Attention

Imagine your teacher spends more time with another student because he needs extra help with spelling. You might feel jealous of him because he is getting more of your teacher's attention than you are. This is another common type of jealousy.

Your jealousy might lead you to get upset or act badly in class. Instead, you should find ways to deal with your feelings. One way to deal is to talk to an adult when you feel jealous.

You and your siblings might feel jealous of each other from time to time. This is natural, but it is important to learn to work out your problems in positive ways.

Siblings

If you have a brother or sister, you likely have had a **sibling rivalry**. This often happens when siblings compete with each other for their parents' attention. They might end up taking their jealousy out on each other and start fighting.

Remember that you and your siblings are different people. You are special in your own ways. You have your own special talents that set you apart from your siblings. Knowing these things will help you begin to feel better about yourself.

Helping out with a new sibling can make you feel a part of your growing family. It can be a positive way to deal with jealous feelings.

A New Baby in the Family

Have you had a new baby brother or sister join your family? If you have, you might have noticed that the baby needs a lot of your parents' attention. You might begin to feel jealous of the new baby. This is another form of sibling rivalry.

It is important to remember that these feelings of anger and jealousy are natural. You should remember that your parents still love you. It might help to talk to them about your feelings about the new baby.

It might help to have some time to yourself to think about why you are having jealous feelings. Understanding your feelings can help you better deal with your feelings.

Recognizing Jealousy

When you feel jealous, you might have other feelings mixed in with the jealousy. You might also feel angry, sad, or **confused**. It is important to **recognize** why you are having these feelings. Did someone have a toy you wanted? Did your teacher pay more attention to your friend during class? If so, then your feelings were caused by jealousy.

Once you know you are feeling jealous, try to put your feelings into words. This will help you understand your jealousy. Understanding jealousy will help you deal with your feelings. Dealing with your feelings will help you feel better.

An adult might help you find positive ways to deal with your feelings. Talking to an adult can also help you let out your feelings and understand them.

Talking About Feeling Jealous

It is important to learn to show your feelings in healthy ways. If you do not, you will become more upset.

Talking with someone you trust about your jealous feelings is one way to deal with them. You should try to talk to an adult. He or she can help you learn to feel better about yourself. Maybe you can find a new sport or a club. If you do something that makes you feel special and good about yourself, it can help keep jealous feelings away.

Finding things that you are good at and that you enjoy can help you turn your jealousy into positive feelings.

Turning It Around

When you feel jealous because of something you do not have, try to remember everything you do have. When you feel jealous because of what someone else can do, think about what you can do. This is a way of turning your jealous feelings into positive feelings.

Everyone has **goals**, dreams, skills, and talents. Finding yours will help you be happy. Keeping jealous feelings to yourself will not make them go away. Talk about them with someone you trust.

Feeling Happy for Someone

Once you know what makes you feel jealous and how to deal with it, it will become easier to feel happy for others. This can make you feel happier because you can share happiness with others.

The next time your friend does something great, tell him or her how happy you are for her or him. This can make it easier for your friend to feel happy for you. Learning to share happiness with others is a positive result of learning to deal with jealousy. Jealousy is a strong feeling, but it does not have to control you!

Glossary

arguments (AR-gyoo-mints) Disagreements.

cheer (CHEER) To clap and shout.

compete (kum-PEET) To play against another in a game or test.

confused (kun-FYOOZD) Mixed up.

goals (GOHLZ) Things that a person wants to do or be.

joins (JOYNZ) Comes together or takes part in.

recognize (reh-kig-NYZ) To know from past knowledge.

rivalry (RY-vul-ree) A struggle between two people or things to see which one is the best.

sibling (SIH-bling) A person's sister or brother.

upset (up-SET) Having hurt feelings.

Index

Web Sites

Due to the changing nature of Internet links, PowerKids Press has developed an online list of Web sites related to the subject of this book. This site is updated regularly. Please use this link to access the list:

www.powerkidslinks.com/lwio/jealousy/